**Unique and Wonderful**

**Written and Illustrated by Dee Smith**

**Copyright © 2016**

**Visit Deesignery.com**

D1530937

Unique and wonderful.

You're one of a kind.

A smile like yours is not easy to find.

Love your hair texture.

Love the color of your skin.

Love that amazing person that lies deep within.

Celebrate yourself and others.

That will take you far.

Let your differences help you shine bright, like a dark night's dazzling star.

Everyone has a different journey.

Choose your own special way.

You can follow your dreams.

You can brighten someone else's day.

The things you may not like about yourself are simply gifts in disguise.

You'll see beauty in them too if you simply open your eyes.

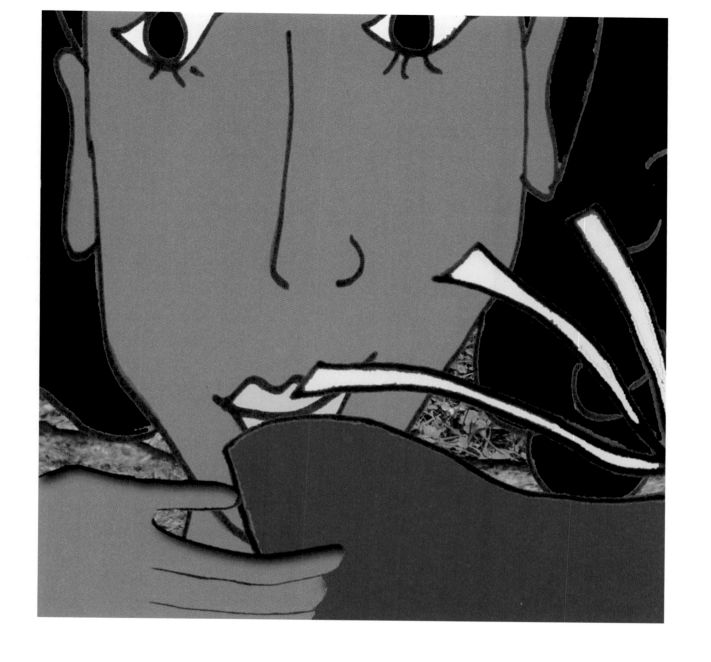

We are all smart and talented in all sorts of unique ways.

Love yourself now.

Don't doubt or delay.

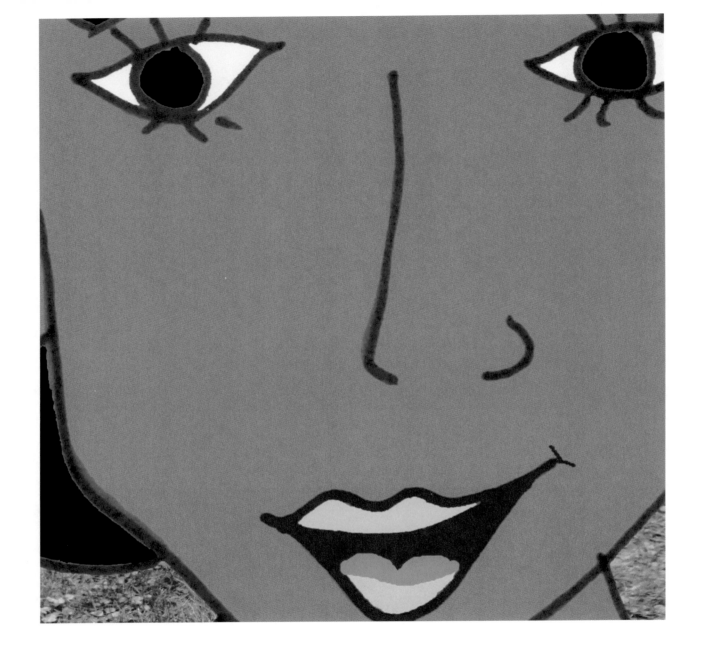

Hey you!

You're one of a kind.

A person just like you is impossible to find.

Dedicated to the Children of Mount Vernon, New York
Thanks for helping me realize some of my closest goals and dreams.

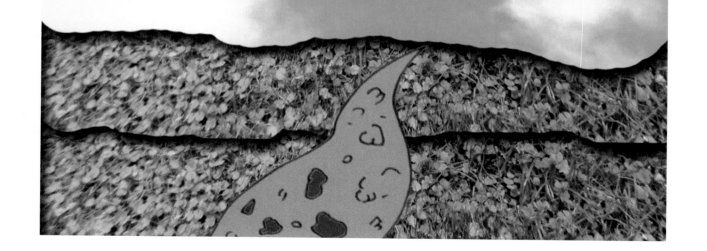

## Thank You!

Thank you so much for reading this book.
It means the world to me!
If you liked the book I would much appreciate if you would write a Review on Amazon. I am so thankful for each and every person supporting my dream of being a writer for children. Because you have read this book, yes that means YOU too! Thanks Again!
Stay tuned for more titles on my website Deesignery.com

Regards,
Dee

## About the Author:

My name is Dee Smith. I am an Author and Illustrator. My hobbies include graphic design, puppetry, balloon twisting, drawing and of course writing. I am dedicated to my mission of keeping children entertained in fun and innovative ways.

Made in the USA
Monee, IL
11 January 2020

20209228R00017